# North Police

# Elf Detectives

Published by Curious Fox, an imprint of Capstone Global Library Limited, 264 Banbury Road, Oxford, OX2 7DY – Registered company number: 6695582

www.curious-fox.com

Text copyright © 2016 Scott Sonneborn
The author's moral rights are hereby asserted.

Illustrations copyright © 2016 Capstone
All characters in this publication are fictitious and any resemblance to real persons, living or dead, is purely coincidental.

ISBN 978-1-78202-609-9
21 20 19 18 17
10 9 8 7 6 5 4 3 2 1

First published as four paperback editions:
Reindeer Games (978-1-4747-0032-0); The Mystery of Santa's Sleigh (978-1-4747-0031-3); Computer Meltdown (978-1-4747-0032-0); Meet the South Police (978-1-4747-0033-7)

A CIP catalogue for this book is available from the British Library.

Printed and bound in China.

THE NORTH POLICE

THE NORTH POLICE

The North Police are

the elves who solve crimes

at the North Pole.

**These are their stories . . .**

# Chapter 1
# Red-nosed reindeer

It was a bright, cold morning in Christmas Town.

In the North Police station, the chief shouted, "Detectives Sprinkles and Sugarplum! Get into my office! Now!"

Sitting beside the chief was
an unhappy reindeer. He had
a shiny red nose.

"What's happened to your
nose?" asked Sugarplum.

"I was playing in the Reindeer Games," said the reindeer. "Then – WHAM! – someone bopped me with a snowboard. I lost the race and got this red mark."

"Now they won't let this red-nosed reindeer join in any Reindeer Games," the chief told Sprinkles and Sugarplum. "Competing when injured is against the rules."

"Whoever wins the Games joins Donner, Blitzen and the others pulling Santa's sleigh," said the reindeer. "I was in first place."

"Do you think another reindeer knocked you out of the Games on purpose?" asked Detective Sugarplum. "This case sounds stickier than a wet candy cane!"

"That's why I'm putting my two best detectives on the case," the chief replied. "I'm sending you both to the Reindeer Games ... undercover!"

## CHAPTER 2
# Reindeer Games

At the Games, two reindeer raced on skates. Another pair wrestled with their antlers.

One reindeer swayed on wobbly legs.

"Hey, look at him!" said
a mean-looking reindeer,
pointing at the wobbly one.

All the other reindeer
laughed and called him
names.

They didn't know it, but there was a good reason the wobbly reindeer couldn't stand up straight. It was the North Police in disguise!

"I don't know if this plan will work," said Sprinkles. "We can't even stand, much less play Reindeer Games!"

"That's why it's going to work." Sugarplum smiled.

The nasty reindeer slid over to them on her snowboard. "Let's race," she said. "You look like you'll be easy to beat!"

The North Police tried to climb onto a snowboard.

"Whoa!" cried Sugarplum and Sprinkles. They slipped and fell into the snow.

"This isn't fair," Detective Sprinkles told the nasty reindeer. "You'll win easily."

"I don't care about fair!" said the nasty reindeer. "I just want to win!"

Lying on the ground, the North Police saw the bottom of the reindeer's snowboard.

It was bright red – except for a nose-shaped mark of missing paint.

"We've caught you red-handed!" said Sugarplum.

ZIPPP! The elves removed their disguise.

"The North Police!" the
nasty reindeer shouted.
And with that, she flew into
the air!

# CHAPTER 3
# The Saint Nick of time

"Roasted chestnuts!" shouted Sprinkles, watching the reindeer zoom away.

Sugarplum flashed her badge. Then she hitched a ride on a nearby reindeer.

The North Police detectives
WHOOOOSHED through the
sky. They soon spotted the
suspect.

"I'm getting too old for
this!" cried Sprinkles.

"Don't be silly," replied Sugarplum. "You're only three hundred and twelve."

She grabbed Sprinkles's arm and jumped!

The North Police landed
on top of the nasty reindeer.
Sugarplum popped handcuffs
onto the reindeer's legs.

"We've done it!" cried
Detective Sprinkles.

"You've done it, all right!"
said the nasty reindeer. "I can't
fly with handcuffs on!"

"Ahhh!" they all shouted,
tumbling out of the sky.

"Ho, ho, hold on!" cried a
voice. It was Santa!

He caught the North Police
and the reindeer in his sleigh.
"Looks like I got here in the
Saint Nick of time!" he said.

"Thanks, Santa," said
Detective Sprinkles.

"Thank you," said Santa. "Without you, I would've had a cheater pulling my sleigh this Christmas."

"Just doing our jobs," said Sugarplum.

"Hooray for the North Police!" said Santa.

"Hooray!" everyone shouted out with glee.

# THE NORTH POLICE

## Santa's Scratched Sleigh

# CHAPTER 1
# Scratched!

The Christmas Town garage is where Santa's sleigh was stored.

It was also a crime scene!

Santa's sleigh had a huge scratch on it.

Someone must have taken the sleigh out last night and scraped it on something.

Santa couldn't have taken the sleigh out. He had been in bed with a cold.

So who did it?

The North Police's greatest detectives were on the case!

As Detective Sugarplum sipped some egg nog, Detective Sprinkles got to work.

Sprinkles dusted for prints with icing sugar.

But there were no fingerprints at all.

"Hmm," said Sugarplum,

"if someone rode the sleigh last night, they would have left prints. Let's talk to the elf who called about the crime."

Eve's job was to look after

Santa's sleigh.

"What can you tell us, Eve?"
asked Sugarplum.

"Only one elf was near the
garage," Eve said. "Elfis."

# CHAPTER 2
# Elfis

Elfis was the coolest elf
in Christmas Town.

The North Police found him
rocking out on his electric bell
at a local Christmas club.

"You were seen near
the garage last night," said
Detective Sprinkles.

"I'm not talking," Elfis said.

"Then you leave us no
choice," said Sugarplum.

"We're going to have to
play good cop, better cop,"
added Sugarplum.

"Go ahead and try," Elfis
said. "Do your best."

"Maybe this will change your mind," said Sprinkles. He held out a bag of candy.

"Jelly beans!" Elfis cried.

"If you want the beans, you'll have to spill the beans," explained Sugarplum.

"I admit it!" said Elfis, grabbing the jelly beans. "I did it! I lost Mrs. Claws!"

"What are you talking about?" asked Sprinkles.

"Santa's cat! I lost her!" said Elfis. "I went looking for her near the garage."

"So you didn't take the sleigh out for a ride?" asked Detective Sprinkles.

"No!" said Elfis.

"Looks like we're out of clues." Sprinkles sighed.

"I don't think so," said Sugarplum. "I think Elfis has just given us another one!"

# CHAPTER 3
# Case closed

The detectives returned to the scene of the crime.

"I bet the sleigh was scratched on the North Pole," said Sprinkles. "That pole is very pointy!"

"But I don't understand how someone could have taken the sleigh out of the garage last night without being seen," Sprinkles said.

"I don't think anyone took the sleigh out," said Sugarplum.

"Then how did it get scratched on the North Pole?" asked Sprinkles.

"It wasn't scratched by
the North Pole," replied
Sugarplum. "Was it, girl?"

"Um, I'm not a girl," replied
a very confused Detective
Sprinkles.

"No, you're not," said Detective Sugarplum, "but she is!" Sugarplum reached behind the sleigh and pulled out ...

a cat!

It was Mrs Claws!

"You scratched the sleigh," said Detective Sugarplum as she petted the cat, "didn't you, girl?"

"Meow," said Mrs Claws.

"Another case neatly wrapped up!" the detectives exclaimed.

The North Police had done it again!

Santa was feeling better and was happy that the case had been solved. He was even happier to have his cat back.

Santa gave Mrs Claws a jolly old hug.

"Achooo!" he sneezed.

"Sir," said Sprinkles, "maybe you're allergic to cats."

"Another mystery for the North Police!" said Sugarplum.

# CHAPTER 1
# Santa's computer

Inside Santa's workshop was a computer. Every day, Santa sat at this computer. Every day, he added names to his naughty and nice lists.

But not today...

Santa's computer was missing!

"It was here yesterday," Santa told the North Police's two greatest detectives. "Now there's just a puddle."

"Christmas is tomorrow,"
said Santa sadly. "How will I
know who should get presents
without my lists? You've got to
find out what's happened to
my computer!"

"Maybe the computer had a meltdown," said Detective Sprinkles. "It is rather warm in here."

"I've never heard of a computer melting into water," said Detective Sugarplum. "But there's one way to find out if that's what happened."

"To the lab!" Sprinkles said.

The North Police scooped
the water into a sandwich bag.
"To all a good night of
crime solving!" exclaimed
Santa as the North Police left.

# CHAPTER 2
# The North Police lab

At the lab, Sprinkles and Sugarplum waited. Their helper elf tested the water.

First, he poured the water into a test tube. Then he put it under a microscope.

"So is it water?" asked Detective Sprinkles.

The helper lifted the test tube and drank the contents.

"Melted snow, to be precise," said the scientist.

"Melted snow!" shouted Detective Sugarplum. "Let's take another look at the crime scene, Sprinkles. I might know what happened to Santa's computer!"

# CHAPTER 3
# Cold case

The two North Police detectives returned to the scene of the crime.

"Look," said Sugarplum, pointing to the floor. "There's more water over here."

"So?" replied Sprinkles. "It's just melted snow."

"Exactly!" said Detective Sugarplum. "And look where it leads..."

The puddles of water led directly to the toilet blocks.

There were three toilet blocks: the women's, the men's and the snowmen's.

WHAM! WHAM! Detective
Sugarplum knocked on the
door to the snowmen's block.

"Open up!" she said. "It's
the North Police!"

There was no answer.

"If there's a snowman in there, button up your coal buttons," said Sugarplum. "We're coming in!"

The two elves burst into the
snowmen's block.

"Brrr," said Sprinkles. "This
isn't like any other toilet block
I've ever seen."

"That's because you're not a snowman," said a voice.

The two North Police detectives turned and saw a snowman. He was holding Santa's computer!

"How did you know I took it?" asked the snowman.

"The melted snow," said Detective Sugarplum. "That's what gave you away."

The snowman nodded.

"It was so hot in Santa's workshop that I started to melt," the snowman said. "So I grabbed the computer and brought it here."

"I knew taking the computer was wrong, but I did it anyway," the snowman said. "I just had to find out if my name was on Santa's list!"

"Well, you're definitely on Santa's list now," said Detective Sprinkles.

"Really?" asked the snowman. "Naughty or nice?"

Sugarplum handcuffed the snowman. "I'll let you work that out," she said.

The North Police smiled.

"Another case neatly wrapped up!" they cheered.

# CHAPTER 1
# Missing!

Detective Sprinkles of the North Police ran into the chief's office.

"Detective Sugarplum has vanished, sir," cried Sprinkles. "She's been missing all day!"

"That's because she's on holiday," replied the chief.

It was the day after Christmas Day. After working so hard on the 25th December, many elves had taken the following day off.

"But what if there's trouble?" Sprinkles worried. "I've never solved a case without a partner."

"You won't have to," said the chief.

"The South Police have sent one of their best officers to help out," the chief explained.

The South Police officer waddled into the room.

"HONK!" he said.

Sprinkles leaned over to the chief. "Sir, that's a penguin," he whispered.

"Of course," said the chief. "That's who lives in the South Pole!"

"All the best officers in the South Police are penguins," the chief added.

"HONK!" agreed the penguin.

Suddenly, the police radio on the chief's desk squawked.

"There's trouble on the Christmas Town ring road!" said a voice over the radio.

# CHAPTER 2
# **Honk!**

The Christmas Town ring road was jammed with elves returning to the North Pole after their day off.

The police sleigh couldn't get through the traffic.

"No problem," said
Sprinkles. "I'll just use my
sleigh bell siren."

Sprinkles hit the button.
Nothing happened.

The siren was broken!

"How will we get through all this traffic?" said Sprinkles.

"HONK!" said the penguin.

"Great idea!" said Detective Sprinkles as the traffic moved out of the way.

Sprinkles and the South Police officer led the tow sleigh to the trouble.

It was Sugarplum! The ice road had cracked under her sleigh. She was stuck!

Suddenly, the ice broke!
Sugarplum's sleigh fell towards
the icy water below.

"Oh no!" cried Sprinkles.
"If she hits the water, she'll be
frozen for sure!"

# CHAPTER 3
# Rescue!

Detective Sprinkles
jumped out of the police sleigh.
He grabbed the tow rope.
Sprinkles threw the rope to
Sugarplum as she fell.
But he missed!

"HONK!" cried the South Police officer.

The penguin dived through the air. He grabbed the rope in his beak.

The penguin hooked the rope onto Sugarplum's sleigh as it fell through the air.

Then the South Police officer splashed down into the freezing water!

The rope caught the
sleigh just in time. Detective
Sugarplum was safe!

But what about the South
Police officer?

"HONK!" said the penguin as he popped out of the water. He was okay, too!

"That water is much too cold for an elf," said Detective Sprinkles.

"But for a penguin,"
Sprinkles added, "I think the
water is just right."

The tow sleigh pulled
Sugarplum and her sleigh back
onto the road.

"I knew you'd get here in time, Detective Sprinkles," Sugarplum said. "The North Police are always there when you need them."

"So are the South Police," added Sprinkles.

"HONK!" agreed the penguin.

The North Police smiled.

"Another case neatly wrapped up!" they cheered.

# CHRISTMAS CRIMINALS

## Spike

**Mrs. Claws**

**Clancy**

## AUTHOR

Scott Sonneborn has written many books, a circus (for Ringling Bros. Barnum & Bailey) and lots of TV programmes. He's been nominated for one Emmy and spent three amazing years working at DC Comics. He lives in Los Angeles, USA, with his wife and their two sons.

## ILLUSTRATOR

Omar Lozano lives in Monterrey, Mexico. He has always been crazy about illustration, constantly on the lookout for awesome things to draw. In his spare time, he watches lots of films, reads fantasy and sci-fi books and draws! Omar has worked for Marvel, DC, IDW, Capstone and many other publishers.